LU, the Little LADYBUG that was afraid to FLY

Idea and words by Yuliya Barannikova

Illustrations by Bohdana Bodnar

For Andriy, Matviy, and Luka
Who are always discovering new things every day

This is the story of a little ladybug called Lu. She loved sitting on her white daisy and gazing up at the clouds in the sky. But she had a secret... Lu had never opened her wings; she had never flown before.

"Today is a wonderful day for flying!" said the other ladybugs as they flew above Lu. "I just love the feeling of the wind beneath my wings!" exclaimed one of the ladybugs.

Hearing that, Lu wanted to fly more than anything in the whole world but she was not ready to open her wings.

"What if I fall from the sky?" she wondered.

It was another beautiful day and Lu was resting on her daisy. Suddenly a strong gust of wind began to blow!

Whoosh Whoosh!

Before she knew it, Lu was carried away by the wind!

"Help!" she cried. "Please! Somebody help me! I can't fly!"

CRAAASH!!!

"Ouch!" cried Lu.

She couldn't see her beloved white daisy, nor the other ladybugs. The little ladybug began to cry little ladybug tears.

"Why are you crying, little ladybug?"

Lu turned around to see a green caterpillar!

"I'm very lost Mr. Caterpillar," sniffled Lu, 'Oh! How I miss my white daisy!"

"Why don't you try flying high above to see your white daisy?" asked Mr. Caterpillar. Lu looked down at her little feet and said in a very small voice "But... I can't open my wings. What if I fall down?"

"I used to be very clumsy when I was learning to crawl! But I practiced over and over and over. Now I'm a GREAT crawler!" exclaimed the caterpillar proudly.

"By the way, I'm good at pushing things! I can push you hard enough so that you try to open your wings and fly"

Lu gave a small smile and said: "I'll give it a try!"

Together the caterpillar and Lu tumbled and bumbled and rumbled and stumbled.

"Flap your wings! You can do it!" called Mr. Caterpillar.

But nothing worked. Lu was still not ready to open her wings...

"By golly, I have an idea!" said Mr. Caterpillar excitedly. "Wait right here! I'll be back in a flash!" he said before crawling into the long grass.

The green caterpillar kept his promise and came back in double-quick time. But this time he was not alone, but with two brown ants.

"These ants are very strong; they can try to lift you and run as fast as possible for your wings to catch the wind and fly" explained Mr. Caterpillar.

Lu gave a small smile and said "I'll give it a try!"

The ants lifted up the ladybug and started to run as fast as their six powerful legs could run.

"Open your wings! You can do it!" encouraged the ants. But Lu was not ready to open her wings.

"We have an idea! Wait right here! We'll be back in double-quick time!" chorused the ants together before scurrying back into the long grass.

When they returned they were not alone, but with a spider with two big eyes.

"Our friend, Mrs. Spider makes the most wonderful webs! They make for great trampolines! You could try jumping on one to practice your flying!" trilled the Ants.

Lu thought it was a wonderful idea. She gave a small smile and said: "I'll give it a try!"

The Spider with two big eyes took Lu and placed her in the middle of her web. And Lu began to jump...

BOING! BOING!

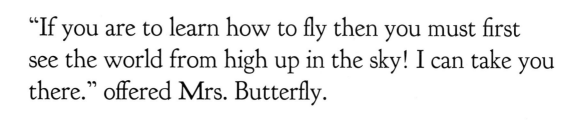

"Open your wings! You can do it!" encouraged Mrs. Spider. But Lu was still not ready to open her wings.

Right at that moment, a gentle voice from high up in the trees said: "I can see that you're having some trouble there, my friends". It was a beautiful Butterfly with large colorful wings.

"If you are to learn how to fly then you must first see the world from high up in the sky! I can take you there." offered Mrs. Butterfly.

Lu didn't feel too sure of Mrs. Butterfly's plan. But oh! How she wanted to see the great world from high up in the sky.

She gave a big smile and said: "I'll give it a try!"

Lu timidly nodded and climbed on the beautiful butterfly's back;

Lu closed her eyes very tightly. She could feel the wind on her 6 little legs. Ever so slowly she peeked open her eyes and was amazed by what she saw...!

From high up in the sky, the little ladybug saw bustling cities filled with people, four-wheeled cars and tall houses which she had never seen before...

Long flowing rivers that looked like long blue ribbons weaving through rolling green hills...

And oh! Mountains! The beautiful mountains with fluffy
white clouds.

They landed on meadow with flowers. The little ladybug jumped off the butterfly's back and flapped her wings with excitement.

"I'm ready to open my wings! I want to try to fly!" she said confidently.

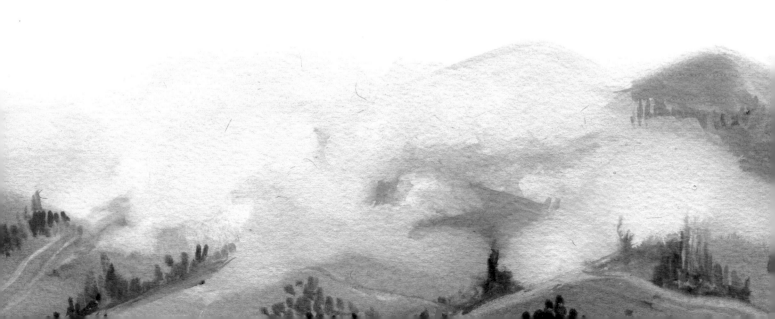

Lu spread her wings as wide as she could. She took a deep breath then took a great big leap from the flower and...before she knew it she was flying!

All of the fear she felt before had melted away. How she soared through the blue skies!

Later that day, Lu flew back home to her white
daisy. She waved to the butterfly and the spider;
she waved to the caterpillar and the ants.

At last, Lu snuggled into the petals of her daisy. "Try, always try." whispered the little ladybug before she finally fell asleep.

This is a story of a little ladybug called Lu. She loved sitting on her daisy and gazing up at the clouds in the sky.

But most of all she loved flying high above the flowers and feeling the air on her tiny but brave wings!

About the Author

Yuliya received a degree in economics in Ukraine and in education management in the US. She worked in a non-governmental sector for six years as a founder of the educational organisation for teacher's professional development in Ukraine. Yuliya the proud mother of three boys who are the inspiration behind her stories. Her sons give her lots of ideas for engaging and meaningful stories every day. They are the first to read her stories and give her helpful feedback. Yuliya loves to share her writing and her journey through motherhood on her social media platforms. She loves spending time outdoors, drinking coffee and spending time with her family.

www.thewayswegrow.com

Follow the Author on Instagram
@the.ways.we.grow

Join on Twitter @AuthorYuliya

More Books about Lu and her Adventures Coming in 2020

If you enjoyed the Ladybug Lu Story leave your feedback on Amazon

ISBN 978-1-7349307-0-2

www.thewayswegrow.com